SHIKARI SHAMBU
Jungle Fever!

WHO? ME?

Shikari Shambu is everything he doesn't appear to be. Just like his name. Although known as Shikari, he is no hunter. He is a conservationist and a wildlife expert. People turn to him in times of crises. Whether it is for rescuing a wild animal or catching a dangerous criminal, this forest ranger is everybody's go-to guy. But, lo and behold, Shambu is no brave heart. He is secretly petrified of animals and has no love for adventure. All he seeks is a good, fluffy pillow to sleep on. But trouble always finds its way to Shambu and luck finds him a way out. And the combination of the two creates a hilarious mad-venture!

Created by former Tinkle Editor, Luis Fernandes, and brought to life by artist V. B. Halbe, Shikari Shambu is one of the most popular characters in the Tinkle stable. For over 30 years, he has had many adventures and run-ins with the wildest and most exotic of animals, birds, insects, plants, and, occasionally, humans. Illustrated by Savio Mascarenhas since 1998, Shambu has only gone from funny to funnier.

I would like to be Shikari Shambu as he gets out of every situation without actually doing anything at all. **– Dhruvraj Singh Rathore,** Jaipur, Rajasthan

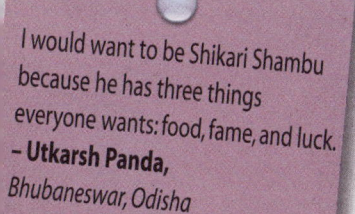

I love Shikari Shambu. He makes *Tinkle* an awesome and all-time-loved magazine for me. I wish Shikari Shambu would come up on TV too! **– Alan Chacko**

I would like to be the hilarious Shikari Shambu because people will praise me for doing nothing. **– Dheeraj Dharman,** Unalur, Kerala

I would want to be Shikari Shambu because he has three things everyone wants: food, fame, and luck. **– Utkarsh Panda,** Bhubaneswar, Odisha

Shambu is a superstar! **– Saurabh Turakhia**

Who wouldn't want to be Shikar Shambu? He has an adventure every day. **– Varun Chindage,** Pune, Maharashtra

I want to be like Shikari Shambu because no matter what he does he always comes out on top. **– Aayush Chetan Salian,** Navi Mumbai, Maharashtra

SHIKARI SHAMBU
GAME ON

Story & Script Shruti Dave
Pencils & Inks Savio Mascarenhas
Colours Umesh Sarode
Letters Pranay Bendre

Fun, adventure, entertainment
Multiplied by 5

Your favourite Tinkle toons are back with lots of stories to keep your spirits high. And if the stories are not enough, you will also find a dash of sports, a pinch of art & craft and a handful of science facts giving you one fun-filled pack!

To buy this Fantastic Five, visit your nearest bookstore or buy online at www.amarchitrakatha.com or call 022-40497417/31/35/36

Shambu & Friends

Shikari Shambu has spent many years in the wild examining and studying all the birds and animals he can find. Shambu has taken a break of late to study human beings. Two particular sets of Tinkle characters have caught his eye. We'll leave it to Shambu to tell you about them.

Defective Detectives: Now these are two boys after my own heart, Rahul and Ravi. They love eating as much as I do. Except, they seem to have a lot of energy, unlike me!

If one were to be unkind, one could also say they are hyperactive. It doesn't help that they are hyper imaginative too! The cases they have invented out of thin air and the messes they have left behind! Now if I were as hyper imaginative and paranoid, why I'd imagine a tiger behind every bush.

Er… do I hear a rustling behind that bush? No? Okay. But I have to admit, I do like all those code names they keep. Agent Crouching Tiger. Agent Hidden Dragon. Agent Hawk Eye. Come to think of it, a lot of these are animal related. I think I hear some growling behind that bush now! Are the boys rubbing off on me?

Coming back to them, the poor things are called the Defective Detectives. What makes it worse is that one of them, Ravi, has a smart sister, Samhita or Sam as they call her. She wanted to join them but has figured out she is better off on her own. To her surprise and frankly even mine, the boys do solve a case now and then! If only they'd learn from my examples, they wouldn't always end up with cake on their faces… mmm… cake!

But what is that rustling? I'd better go check… or rather scoot! Bye!

Ina Mina Mynah Mo: Now let me introduce you to Ina, Mina, Mynah and Mo. Just saying their names exhausts me.

I don't know how their parents, Jagannath and Bina keep up with them.

Look at Ina. The girl changes clothes as often as a chameleon in the wild changes colours. She reminds of a peacock, always happy to display her magnificent feathers.

Then we have Mina. The poor girl can't ever make up her mind. Which perhaps explains why she's so bossed around by her sisters!

We then have Mynah, who is quite headstrong, a bookworm and an aggressive activist for causes big and small.

Mo is the youngest. She loves to cook and eat, just like me, except for the cooking part of course.

Speaking of cooking, we also have Bina, mother to all these girls and quite the cook herself.

Last but definitely not the least is Jagannath. Jaggu, as he's fondly known, is like always nagging everybody and always, always worried about money.

That's all then, phew! What a large family they are.

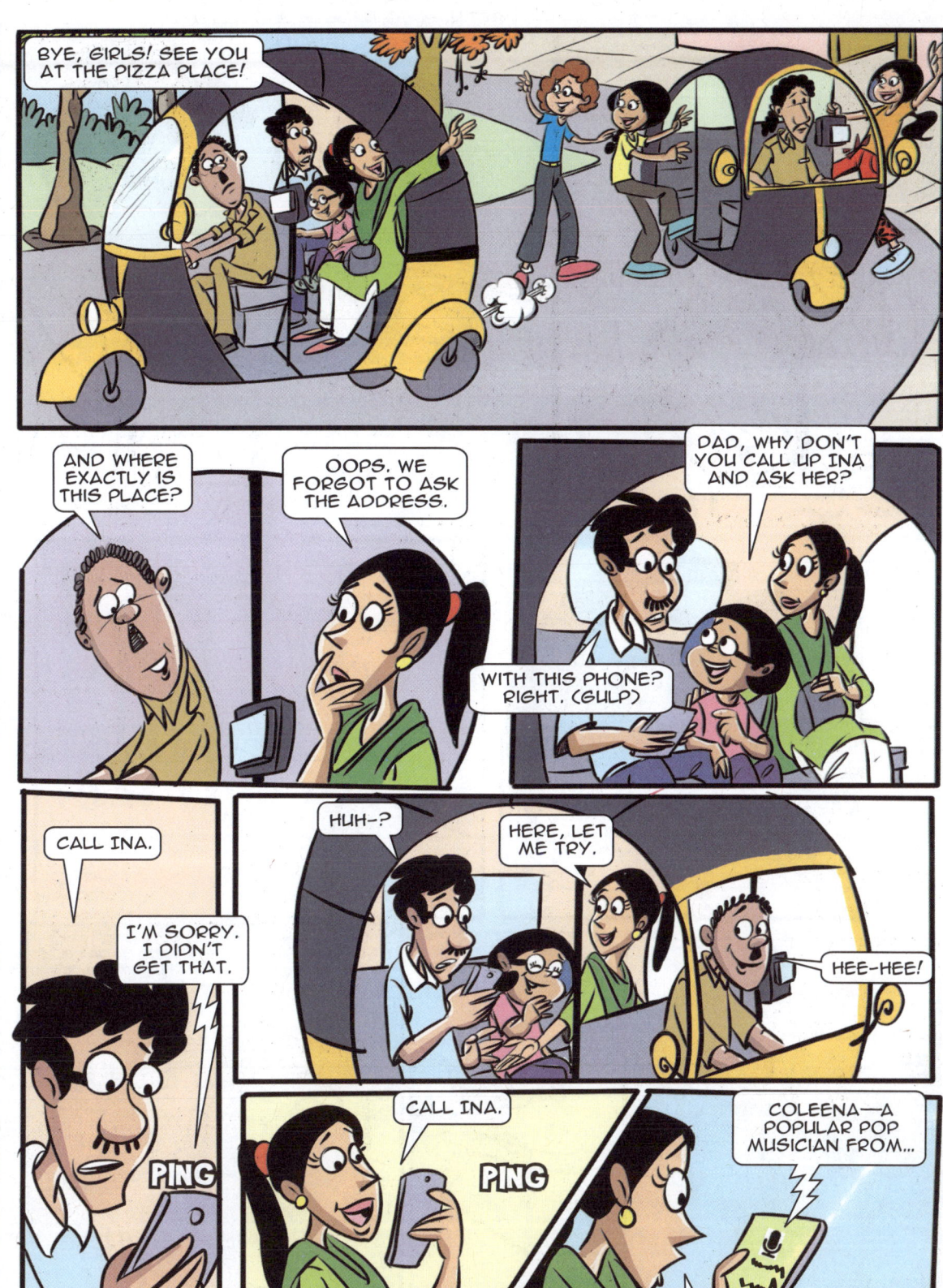

Shikari Shambu — SURVIVAL OF THE FITTEST

Story & Script Sean D'mello
Pencils & Inks Savio Mascarenhas
Colours Snehangshu & Vineet
Letters Snehangshu Mazumder

I'M GLAD YOU ASKED, SHAMBU. THERE ARE THREE CONTESTS TODAY. THE CONTESTANT WHO WINS TWO OF THESE WILL BE CROWNED 'THE GREATEST SURVIVOR'.
I DO HOPE WE'LL BE DONE BEFORE MY SIESTA!
"FOR OUR FIRST CONTEST, BOTH OUR DAREDEVILS WILL BE TASKED WITH COLLECTING HONEY FROM A HOSTILE BEEHIVE."
SHOULD BE EASY ENOUGH. SHAMBU IS **PETRIFIED** OF BEES.
BEES? OH NO...
OFF THEY GO! JJ SEEMS TO HAVE TAKEN THE LEAD. I WONDER WHAT'S SLOWING SHAMBU DOWN.
I WAS RIGHT. LOOK AT SHAMBU—HE IS SCARED STIFF.
BAA!

SHAMBU HAS SOMEHOW CAUGHT UP WITH JJ. NOW WHOEVER RETRIEVES THE HONEY AND RETURNS FIRST, WILL BE OUR WINNER.
I DON'T GET IT. I THOUGHT HE WAS SCARED OF BEES.
BEES SURE ARE SCARY BUT HONEY... YUM!
SLURP
THEY'VE BOTH GOT THE HONEY AND ARE NOW MAKING THEIR WAY BACK. THIS IS GOING TO BE CLOSE.
"BUT WAIT A MINUTE, WHAT IS THIS? SHAMBU HAS STOPPED BEFORE THE FINISH LINE."
HONEY, I LOVE HONEY!
FINISH LINE
THE MAN HAS FINALLY LOST IT.
THIS IS THE MOST BIZARRE THING I'VE EVER SEEN. THE WINNER OF OUR FIRST CONTEST IS JJ!

FOR OUR SECOND CONTEST WE'VE DROPPED BOTH OUR CONTESTANTS IN THE MIDDLE OF A FOREST. LET'S SEE HOW OUR HUNTERS DEAL WITH A WILD BEAR ON THE LOOSE.
WELL, LOOKS LIKE THE COMPETITION IS ALL BUT OVER. SHAMBU'S MIDDLE NAME IS PANIC.
A B-B-BEAR?!
SOON—
(YAWN!) THAT LUNCH SHANTI HAD PACKED FOR ME FOLLOWED BY ALL THAT HONEY IS MAKING ME SLEEPY. MAYBE I SHOULD LIE DOWN FOR A WHILE.
JUST... FOR 10... MINUTES.
"THERE GOES THE BEAR. HE IS MAKING HIS WAY TOWARDS SHAMBU. I CAN'T WATCH!
THAT FOOL DOESN'T REALIZE HOW CLOSE THE BEAR IS TO HIM.
"OUR FEARLESS SHAMBU HAS ADOPTED THE 'PLAYING DEAD' TECHNIQUE. I MUST SAY, STAYING SO STILL TAKES SOME NERVE.
OH NO! THAT BIG BEAR IS LOOKING MY WAY!

"OUR BEAR HAS NOW TURNED HIS ATTENTION TO JJ WHO SUDDENLY LOOKS FIVE SHADES WHITER. I WONDER HOW LONG IT WILL BE BEFORE HE CALLS FOR HELP.
GROWL!
MUMMY! TAKE HIM AWAY! DO YOU HEAR ME. I CAN'T BEAR THIS.
RAWWWR
"I GUESS THAT'S THE END OF THIS CONTEST. JJ HAS THROWN IN THE TOWEL WHILE OUR DAREDEVIL SHAMBU CONTINUES TO PLAY DEAD."
NOW FOR THE FINAL CONTEST. WE'VE PLACED A HUGE PEARL INSIDE A GIGANTIC OYSTER AT THE BOTTOM OF THE CORAL REEF. THE FIRST MAN TO RETRIEVE THAT PEARL WILL BE CROWNED THE GREATEST SURVIVOR. SO GET SET...
"...GO...
"...GOING...
"...GONE!"
SPLASH!

I CAN'T LOSE TO SHAMBU. NOT WHEN THE WHOLE WORLD IS WATCHING.

I HAVE TO MAKE SURE THAT SHAMBU IS TAKEN OUT OF THE EQUATION ONCE AND FOR ALL. BUT HOW?

I KNOW! I'LL CUT OFF HIS OXYGEN SUPPLY VALVE. THAT WILL TAKE CARE OF HIM.

THIS IS IT! GOODBYE, MR. SHAMBU.
WOAHHHH!
FIZZ
AND OFF HE GOES!
ELSEWHERE...
OH, LOOK... DINNER!
AAAAA
UH-OH... THE FISH WON'T GO DOWN.
COUGH-COUGH!
WHAM!
AH, I CAN BREATHE AGAIN.
PHEW!
I MUST GO THANK THAT MAN WHO SAVED MY LIFE.
AHHHH!

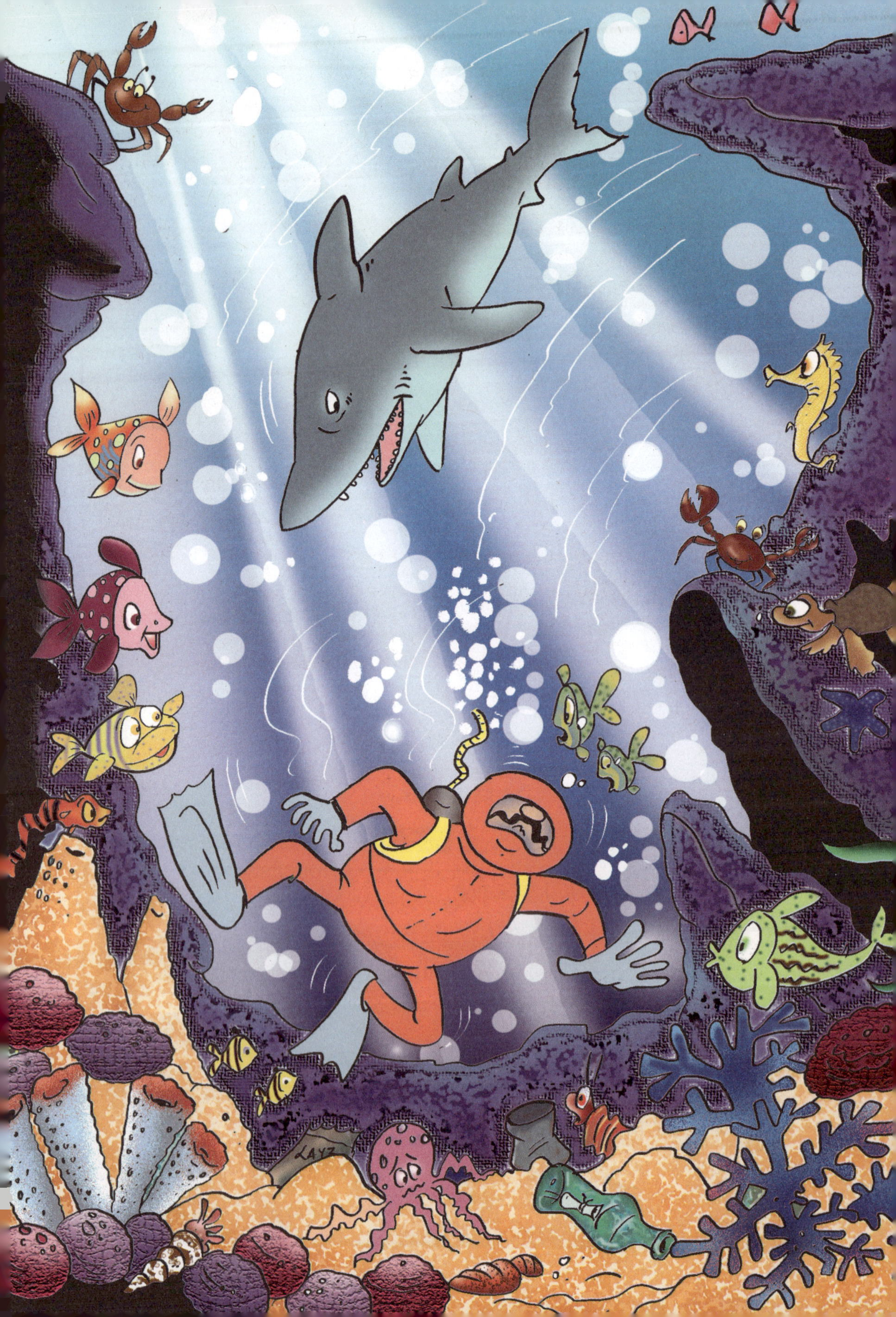

MEANWHILE, JJ REACHES THE BOTTOM OF THE REEF AND...
COME TO ME, MY PRECIOUS!
WOAHHH!
I'VE GOT IT, IT'S ALL MINE.
WHAM!
MY GOD! MY SAVIOUR HAS PASSED OUT... I MUST GET HIM TO THE SURFACE.
OUT OF MY WAY!

WAIT A MINUTE! I THINK I SEE SOME MOVEMENT. ONE OF OUR DAREDEVILS IS RETURNING. WHO DO YOU THINK IT IS?

THAT IS IT! WE HAVE OUR WINNER. CONGRATS, SHAMBU YOU ARE A...

SHARK!

47

SHIKARI SHAMBU
RESCUING DAISY

Writer: **Sharmistha Sinha**
Illustrator: **Savio Mascarenhas**
Colourist: **Shailee**
Letterer: **Gajoo Tayde**

AN UNIDENTIFIED PLANE CRASHED INTO A HIMALAYAN JUNGLE.

A WEEK LATER, AT THE MARKET PLACE...

MR. SHAMBU, MR. SHAMBU...

OH NO! IT'S THE MAD PROFESSOR WHO SENT ME TO BHUTAN TO LOOK FOR A YETI.

AUTO!!

VROOOOM...
AT HOME...
SHANTI... PACK YOUR BAGS. LET'S GO.
BEFORE THE PROFESSOR GETS HERE.
BUT... WHERE ARE WE GOING?
TO YOUR BROTHER'S VILLAGE IN KAMLI.
VROOOOM...
AFTER THREE DAYS OF A BUMPY RIDE, THEY REACHED KAMLI, A VILLAGE IN THE HIMALAYAN FOOTHILLS.
AH! SUCH PEACE AND QUIET...

SUDDENLY...
AAAAAAAA AAAHHHH!!
WAAH WAAH... MY BALL... IT'S TAKEN MY BALL.
RUNNNNN... MONSTER...
HELP!
HUMPH!
BUMP!
OH MR. SHAMBU! I CAME TO MEET YOU. YOUR NEIGHBOUR TOLD ME YOU'D COME HERE. I NEED YOUR HELP...
OH NO!
SHAMBU! BROTHER-IN-LAW!!! YOU'VE COME! JUST IN TIME!
HUH?

STOP! STOP! THIS IS MY BROTHER-IN-LAW – THE GREAT SHIKARI SHAMBU. HE HAS COME TO SAVE US FROM THE MONSTER.
NOOOOOOOOO!!!
WAIT! DON'T GO THAT SIDE... THE MONSTER...
I'D BETTER LEAVE FAST!
HE HAS GONE INTO THE FOREST TO CATCH THE BEAST! COME ON, LET'S FOLLOW HIM.
OH, THE BRAVE MAN!
INSIDE THE FOREST...
KUKKU
KUKKU
HOOOWL
(PANT! PANT!) SAFE AT LAST...
SUDDENLY...
THAACK!!
OOOH! BANANAS!

AAAEEE AAAEEE AAAAAAAEEEEIIII...
AAAEEE AAAEEE AAAAAAAEEEEIIII...
IT'S GOT HIM! THAT WAY, QUICK!
HELP!
HEY! NOT BAD! I'M FLYING!

THAAP!
OUCH!
EEEEEEEEKKKKKS!!
EEEEEEEEKKKKKS!!
WHERE IS IT GOING?
RUN, SHAMBU! NOW!
THAACK!
CLAP!
CLAP!
CLAP!

TAKE THAT, YOU MONKEY!
SOON...
OH! IT'S ENJOYING THAT. AS LONG AS I PLAY, IT WILL NOT HARM ME...
MEANWHILE...
AN AIRCRAFT! GOSH!
YES, MEMSAHIB. ONE WEEK BACK, **BOOM BOOM** IN SKY. TWO MEN IN PARACHUTE FALL IN VILLAGE AND RUN AWAY.
HOLY MACKEREL! A BROKEN CAGE!
IT WAS CARRYING AN ANIMAL! COULD IT BE...?

MEMSAHIB, WE BETTER GO. OTHERS WALK FAR.
RAMU, WHAT DOES THIS MONSTER LOOK LIKE?
OH MEMSAHIB, IT'S TALL LIKE A COCONUT PALM... LONG SHARP NAILS... CROOKED TOES...
BLOODSHOT EYES... FLAMES AROUND ITS BODY...
FLAMES?!!
LIAR! HAVE YOU EVER SEEN IT?
HAVE YOU?
STOP FIGHTING... HAS ANYONE HERE SEEN THE CREATURE?
NO, MEMSAHIB. BUT, MY WIFE'S BROTHER'S FRIEND...
THAT'S ENOUGH!
SOON, THEY REACHED THE TOP OF THE HILLOCK...
!!!
!!!

HE'S TAMED THE MONSTER! HE'S A LIONHEART!
MY BROTHER-IN-LAW, AFTER ALL!
!!!
THEN THE MOST EXTRAORDINARY THING HAPPENED...
EEEEEAAAAAAAA...
MMMUUUAAAAAAAHH!
OH MY DAISY... MY BABY... MY MUNCHKIN...
DAISY!?
BAD MEN KIDNAPPED YOU, DID THEY? TOOK YOU OFF ON A PLANE?
BUT THE PLANE CRASHED AND YOU ESCAPED, DIDN'T YOU? MY SMART KITTY...

THE NEXT DAY, IN THE NEWSPAPERS...

Rare giant orangutan rescued by genius jungle-man, Shikari Shambu

■ Sayoni Basu

GUDGAON: Six months ago, the scientific world was in an uproar when famous ape expert Janice Goodone discovered an unusually large 8 foot orangutan in the Borneo forest. Janice called him 'Daisy'. However, Daisy fell prey to poachers and...

■ Shikari Shambu with Janice Goodone and Daisy
Photo Courtesy JTI

Shikari Shambu: The Man Who Hunts Poachers

Writer	Pencils & Inks	Colours	Letters
Tushar Abhichandani	Savio Mascarenhas	Umesh Sarode	Prasad Sawant

TWO HOURS LATER—

"THIS HAD BETTER BE A GOOD SURPRISE."

ANOTHER HOUR WENT BY—

"I FEEL LIKE WE HAVE BEEN MISLED, MR. SHAMBU. EXPERTS DON'T TAKE THIS LONG TO TRACK WILD ANIMALS!"

"I AGREE. YOU HAVE—"

"YEAH, WE HAVEN'T TAKEN A SINGLE PHOTO YET."

BUT THEN—

"HAH! LOOK AT THAT!"

"IT'S A SLOTH BEAR!"

"I'LL QUICKLY TAKE SOME SHOTS BEFORE HE WAKES UP."

"I AM SORRY, MR. SHAMBU. IT WAS A MISTAKE TO QUESTION YOU."

"DON'T WORRY ABOUT IT. THIS PLACE CAN CONFUSE PEOPLE."

"THAT WAS CLOSE! THANKS, SLOTH BEAR!"

click

59

BUT THEN—
CRACK
HUH?
GRRR
YIKES! HE'S AWAKE! RUN!
MR. SHAMBU! WHY DID YOU WAKE HIM?
UH... IT WAS TIME FOR HIM TO EXCERCISE. HE'D BEEN SLEEPING TOO MUCH, YOU SEE. HEH-HEH.
AND THEY SET OFF ONCE AGAIN—
WE WILL SOON REACH ANOTHER INTERESTING SITE...
...I HOPE.

BUT THE SEARCH PROVED TO BE FUTILE —
HMPH! MR. SHAMBU, WE ARE VERY DISAPPOINTED.
YOU HAVE WASTED OUR DAY!
BUT... LOOK THERE!
FINALLY, WE HAVE A RARE SIGHTING. GET SOME PHOTOS, QUICKLY!
OW! I HAVE NEVER SEEN O MANY BARASINGHAS OGETHER BEFORE. THEY LOOK BEAUTIFUL!
POLOGIES AGAIN, R. SHAMBU. THIS EAT HAS RAISED OUR TEMPERS.
THAT'S ALL RIGHT! I HAVE A LOT OF EXPERIENCE WITH IMPATIENT PHOTOGRAPHERS.
SLAP
SPLASH!
WAAAH!
WHOOPS! SORRY! MY BAD.
CLOP
CLOP
CLOP
URGH!

YOU ARE THE CLUMSIEST WILDLIFE CONSERVATIONIST I HAVE EVER MET!
LET'S GO BACK.
EEP!
I DON'T THINK WE'LL GET ANY MORE PHOTOS OF WILDLIFE IF MR. SHAMBU KEEPS DISTURBING THEM!
BUT SHAMBU'S LUCK HADN'T RUN OUT YET—
OOOH! TIGER CUBS!
CLICK
THIS TIME THE CREW TOOK NO CHANCES—
PLEASE STAY THERE AND DON'T MOVE. I CAN'T AFFORD TO MISS THIS SHOT.
UM... OKAY.

AAH! REST AT LAST!
SUDDENLY—
WAAAAH!
ROAR!
HUH? WHAT'S HE DOING?
AAH!
NO! LEAVE ME ALONE, YOU BAD CAT!
SPRING
CRASH!
UFF!

"MY WORD, MR. SHAMBU! WE MISUNDERSTOOD YOU. YOU WERE TRYING TO FIND THE POACHER ALL ALONG! NO WONDER YOU WERE SO DISTRACTED."

"UH... OF COURSE, OF COURSE! SOMETIMES SUCH MISSIONS REQUIRE DISCRETION. I'M GLAD WE MANAGED TO SAVE THE TIGERS TODAY."

A MONTH LATER—

NATIONAL ECOLOGY MAGAZINE

SHAMBU THE POACHER HUNTER

"POACHER HUNTER? THANK GOODNESS! I MAY NOT BE MARRIED TO THE SMARTEST MAN IN THE WORLD BUT I AM DEFINITELY MARRIED TO THE LUCKIEST!"

(CHOMP-CHOMP) YOU SAID IT. (GULP)

SHIKARI SHAMBU: THE DACOIT

Writer Tushar Abhichandani | **Pencils & Inks** Savio Mascarenhas | **Colours** Akshay Khadilkar | **Letters** Pranay Bendre

HU-HU-HU. THANK GOD! I HOPE THE DACOIT HAS PASSED THE AREA BY NOW.
UNFORTUNATELY—
CLIP
CLOP
OH NO!
HAHAHA... LOOK WHO WE'VE FOUND. IT'S THE FAMOUS SHIKARI SHAMBU. THE LAST TIME WE MET, YOU SPOILT MY PLAN TO POACH SOME LEOPARDS. THIS TIME I WILL POACH **YOU**!

SOON—

HOW DO I ALWAYS END UP IN THESE SITUATIONS?

OUR HELPER RECENTLY FELL ILL, SO NOW YOU'LL HAVE TO DO ALL THE HOUSEWORK FOR OUR CAMP.

ULP!

AND SO—

67

AFTER A LONG AND TIRING DAY IN CAPTIVITY—
WHAT HAS BECOME OF ME? I MISS MY LIFE! AND I CAN'T BELIEVE I'M SAYING THIS, BUT I MISS MY WIFE TOO.
SNIFF
SNORT
WHAT WAS THAT?
THE HORSE! IT LOOKS ILL.
SNORT

OH... THE POOR THING HAS AN INFECTION. THE HORRIBLE DACOITS WON'T EVEN TAKE CARE OF YOU. SO SAD!

SHAMBU DECIDED TO HELP—

I REMEMBER PROFESSOR DAMLE ONCE USED THESE LEAVES TO CURE A HORSE'S INFECTION.

I HOPE IT WORKS.

YOU WANT ME TO RIDE YOU? REALLY? ALL RIGHT, IF YOU INSIST.
I'M HAVING FUN AFTER SO LONG. THANK YOU, MY FRIEND.
BUT THEN—
WAIT! WHAT ARE YOU DOING? WE WILL CRASH INTO THE WALL!
WAAAAAH!
SHAMBU IS GETTING AWAY!

WE WILL GET YOU, SHAMBU. THERE IS NO ESCAPE.
JUST THEN—
OH! SHAMBU! WE'VE BEEN LOOKING FOR YOU. YOU—OH! YOU FOUND BAGGA AND HIS GANG!
POLICE
CAPTURE THEM!
UH-OH!
THE NEXT DAY—
THE GREAT SHIKARI SHAMBU HAS RETURNED.
NOT ONLY DID HE ESCAPE THE CLUTCHES OF BAGGA, HE HELPED CAPTURE HIM TOO!
YES, BUT HE WON'T ESCAPE **MY** CLUTCHES. HE HAS TO ANSWER FOR LEAVING HIS WIFE BEHIND AND RUNNING AWAY!